Raiders Versus Sharks

By Paul Collins

Illustrated by Martin Chatterton

Pearson Australia
(a division of Pearson Australia Group Pty Ltd)
707 Collins Street, Melbourne, Victoria 3008
PO Box 23360, Melbourne, Victoria 8012
www.pearson.com.au

First published 2012 by Pearson Australia
2019 2018 2017 2016
10 9 8 7 6 5 4 3 2

Commissioning Editor: Sabine Bolick
Project Editor: Suzy Freeman
Editor: Sophie Ayerbe
Designer: Anne Donald
Copyright & Pictures Editor: Marg Barber
Illustrator: Martin Chatterton
Printed in Australia by the SOS Print + Media Group

ISBN 978 1 4425 3766 8

Pearson Australia Group Pty Ltd ABN 40 004 245 943

Contents

Chapter 1

A Great Idea

Carl was still smarting about losing the street hockey match to the **Sharks**. He sat up and flicked a curver. The frisbee spun off at a crazy angle but Zeus leapt up, his legs treading air.

Snap! The dog's jaws grabbed the spinning plastic and landed with a thump. He trotted over to his owner and dropped the frisbee at his feet.

"That's it, Zeus, I'm tired!" Carl had been throwing the frisbee for an hour.

Zeus gave a short bark. Carl swung his wheelchair around and saw Genji, Thea and Harrison wandering into his backyard.

"Cool, frisbee!" Thea's eyes widened. "Let's see who can throw it the furthest!"

"The highest!" Harrison suggested.

"The fastest!" Genji added.

Carl flicked the tooth-marked frisbee to Thea, who caught it. Her mouth gaped. "Yuck, Carl. It's full of dog slobber!" She threw it to Harrison, who caught it before he realised what Thea had said.

Zeus looked pleadingly at Harrison. His tail wagged excitedly in hope.

"Don't look at me," Harrison said, throwing the frisbee to Genji. Genji rubbed Zeus behind his ears. "You can get it next time. We don't want you to beat us too."

"So what brings you here?" asked Carl.

Thea laughed. "My brother gave our ferrets some ice cubes to play ice hockey with, and Dad didn't like all the water on the kitchen floor. He's not very happy."

Genji rolled her eyes. "We've all been told to do something 'useful'. At my house that usually means helping to clean the house or wash the car."

Harrison heaved a sigh. "My dad's watching cricket on TV. We were supposed to be going to your dad's shop, Carl, to look at new bikes. Dad said he'd think about buying me a new Five Star bike for my birthday. It's a racing bike like the ones they use in the Tour de France, the greatest bike race in the world."

Carl raised an eyebrow.

"Well … it's by the same company," Harrison added before Carl could correct him. "Let's play a game," he added, changing the subject.

"How about basketball?" Thea suggested.

"It's too hot," Genji said, fanning her face with her hand.

"We could go for a bike ride," Carl said.

"Or we could build a BMX track," Genji said excitedly.

"As if," Harrison said.

Genji put her hands on her hips. "It would only take a few spades and wheelbarrows. We could dig deep holes and make big mounds."

"That's a great idea," Carl said, looking at the paddock next door to his house. "But where would we build it? The last time Mr Coltson let us in his paddock, we trod on some of his potatoes by mistake. No way is he going to let us make a BMX track."

"Besides, the **Sharks** would probably come and take it over," Thea said gloomily.

Genji crossed her arms. "I still can't believe they beat us at street hockey yesterday. Those guys think they're so good. I'd love to beat them at something. Just once!"

She looked at the others. “A bike race would make a great challenge! They might’ve beaten us at street hockey—”

“And everything else,” Thea interrupted.

“Well, I bet we’re faster on our bikes!” Genji finished.

Chapter 2

The Challenge

"A bike race! Twenty laps of Ramsden Oval," Carl said. "That's a cool idea!"

Genji smiled. "Oh, I have them every now and then."

"And we have the perfect coach!" Harrison said. "No-one knows wheels like you, Carl!"

Carl grinned. "You bet. This race is ours, my friends. There's no way the **Sharks** can beat us in a bike race!"

"How can we get them to take us on?" Genji wondered aloud and frowned.

"I reckon we should put ads in the local paper," Harrison said. "We could have a five-dollar entry fee, and the winner gets half of the entry money!"

"Ads cost a lot of money," Carl said. "And I don't think our parents would like the idea of us making money like that."

Thea nodded in agreement. "But the **Sharks** think they're so good at everything, they'll just agree! Especially after yesterday's street hockey match."

"But they cheated!" Harrison said. "They had a ring-in. Mozzie's brother Tye plays in the Juniors' state team. If he hadn't played for them, we'd have beaten them for sure."

"Who cares about hockey?" Genji said. "Why don't we just challenge them like they challenged us when they knew Tye was going to be around yesterday?"

"Right," Carl said, glancing at his friends. "Let's write a challenge!"

Chapter 3

Eat Our Dust!

Carl read out the result of everyone's ideas.

We, the Ramsden Raiders,
challenge the Shelford Sharks
to a 20-lap bike race.
October 11th at 10 a.m. sharp
Ramsden Oval

"We need a really good motto," Genji said. "How about, 'We ride fast, so you won't last!'?"

"Sounds good to me," Carl said, adding the motto to the challenge.

"And one last thing," Harrison said. "Eat our dust."

Carl jotted that down too.

"What about a chant?" Thea suggested. "I could come up with something."

"Good idea, Thea!" Genji said. "That'd be awesome. My sister Lucy and her friends could perform it on the day."

"I hope the **Sharks** don't cheat." Thea rubbed her shoulder. "They were so rough at hockey. I'm still sore."

"We could invite our parents," Harrison offered. "The **Sharks** would have to watch themselves, then!"

"But that would make us look scared," Genji said. "And I'm not scared of them!"

Carl clicked his fingers. "I know! We'll invite spectators. Just like a real race. There's no way the **Sharks** could cheat with lots of people watching!"

"And then our parents could come," added Thea excitedly.

"We'll need posters to put up and pamphlets to hand out," Harrison said.

"We'll put them up on every shop in Shelford Street," Genji said. "That way the **Sharks** can't miss them, and the race will be on!"

Chapter 4

Chickens or Sharks?

Thea, Harrison and Genji met at Carl's place the next day.

"Did you print out the flyers?" Thea asked Carl. She couldn't wait to get started.

"I sure did," he replied. "Take a look." He handed out a bunch of posters and flyers to his friends.

"Cool!" Genji was impressed.

"Let's go and put them up now!" said Harrison.

Carl threw Genji a roll of sticky tape. "Okay, Thea and I will go that way," he said, pointing, "and you and Harry go that way. The **Sharks** will have to accept our challenge or the whole neighbourhood will know they're chickens and not sharks!"

Carl looked at his watch. "Let's meet back here at 2 p.m."

🚲 🚲 🚲

"What took you guys so long?" Thea said to Harrison and Genji, stepping off the porch. She was holding a cold drink. Harrison's eyes narrowed.

"Carl darling, I forgot to tell you, there's a phone message for you," Carl's mum called from the kitchen.

"I bet it's the **Sharks**!" Thea said.

Carl hurried up the ramp and through the front door. He waved his friends into the family room.

"Look who it's from!"

Carl,
Ring Leo Humphries
5743211.

Carl's friends crowded around him as he phoned Leo.

"Well, what do you reckon?" Carl said when Leo answered the phone. "Are you chickens or are you sharks?"

"The **Raiders** don't stand a chance," replied Leo. "I thought you'd have learnt your lesson from street hockey, Carl. And basketball. And soccer." He laughed.

"But if not … the **Sharks** accept your challenge." He hung up.

"Yes!" Carl said, punching the air. "We've got the **Sharks**!"

"What did he say?" Thea asked.

"He sounded scared," Carl said, smiling. "He wanted to only race ten laps 'cause they won't be able to finish!"

"Come on Carl. What did he really say?" asked Thea.

Carl shrugged. "Not much. They accept the challenge."

Carl's mum walked past. "Challenge? What challenge?" she asked.

"Oh, just another game, Mum," Carl said. "I reckon the whole neighbourhood will be there this time."

"You just be careful," Carl's mum looked at them. "What is it this time? Basketball? Rugby? Tennis?"

"A bike race. First team to complete twenty laps of Ramsden Oval."

Carl's mum nodded and walked off. "That's all right then."

"We only have a week to practise," Thea said, wringing her hands. "Will that be enough time?"

All eyes turned to Carl, who smiled. "Well, I have been watching clips of the Tour de France on the Internet. "

"And?" prompted Genji.

Carl frowned. "The Tour de France is over 3400 kilometres long. It runs for twenty-two days every year in France. Cadel Evans was the first Aussie to win it! Bike racing is all about having a strong plan and teamwork. It can be pretty dangerous, and we know the **Sharks** are rough."

Thea shook her head. "Aren't we just riding our bikes as fast as we can?"

"Well, yes, but there's more to it than that," Carl said. "First up, when people overtake, they can sometimes clip the riders they're overtaking. They're not allowed to do this, but sometimes it happens."

"What else?" asked Harrison.

"Once they're in front, the teams bunch up to save energy, and they don't let anyone overtake. So what we need is a race plan and lots of practice," Carl finished.

Chapter 5

Surprise, Surprise!

The Raiders practised hard all week. Carl was a tough coach. Everyone took it in turns to lead the pack around the course. Harrison was the fastest, with Genji a close second.

With only a few days to go, the **Raiders** heard that the **Sharks** had also been training hard.

"Maybe we won't be able to beat them," Genji worried.

Carl shook his head. "You haven't heard my big surprise. What sort of shop does my dad own, guys?"

"A bike shop," answered Genji.

Carl smiled hugely. "Dad just got a new shipment of racing bikes in."

"So we're getting new racing bikes?" Harrison gasped.

"Um ... not exactly," Carl admitted. "But Dad's been testing out one of the new bikes on the sprint track. And guess what? He's booked the track for the race!"

Harrison sighed. "What's so good about the sprint track?"

"It's spot-on for our bike race," answered Carl. "It has marked lanes and spectators can watch. Maybe even a TV crew will come! And Dad said if we all help count stuff in the shop for the stocktake, he'll give Harry's dad a discount on a racing bike for Harry's birthday."

"Yes!" they all yelled.

The next two days were the busiest the **Raiders** had ever had. Every spare moment was spent practising on the sprint track, printing and sticking posters in shops and on notice boards, and helping with the stocktake. This meant counting every single thing in Carl's dad's bike shop.

"Well, if this is what work's all about, I don't think I ever want to leave school," complained Harrison. "Your dad has 484 bike pumps, Carl!"

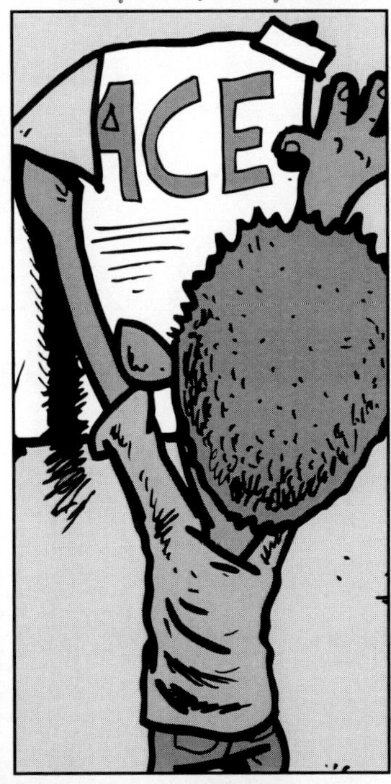
ACE

Carl looked up from where he was counting tyres. "Just keep looking up at that bike," he said, pointing to the Five Star in the shop. "Dad says it helps to have a goal when you're working."

Thea wrote down the number of bicycle chains she had just counted. "Mum said she'd take me shopping after the race. What about you Genji?"

"I'm focusing on the look on the **Sharks'** faces when we beat them tomorrow," Genji said.

Just then, Carl's dad poked his head around the corner. "Your bike race is bringing so many new customers into the shop, I'm thinking of holding a race every year. You guys have done an amazing job with the stocktake too. How about new helmets, tops and racing gloves for the race?"

"Wow, thanks Mr Hedron! We'll really look like pros," they chorused.

"So what are you lot still doing here? Go on, get to that track! You've only got this afternoon to practise. I'll see you all tomorrow!" he smiled.

Chapter 6

And the Winners Are...

Hundreds of people turned up to see the race. Carl wheeled his way through the crowd, stopping next to his father. "Hey Dad, there's Genji's sister Lucy and her friends. They've made up a cheer for us. Is the microphone all set up?"

"Sure is," his dad replied. He waved Lucy over and handed her a mike. "Okay everyone. Sing your hearts out."

Carl's mum stood back and took a photo as they sang into the microphone.

"We ride fast
We've got you sussed
You won't last
So eat our dust!"

Everyone clapped and cameras clicked. Carl's dad took back the microphone. "And now, ladies and gentlemen, boys and girls, the moment you have all waited for... **Raiders versus Sharks**, brought to you by Hedron Bikes!"

Carl's dad held up the starting flag. The cyclists hunched over their bikes, feet itching to pedal.

"Three... two... one..." Carl's dad called, and then he waved the flag.

Harrison's bike streaked ahead. He led the pack for most of the first lap. Carl had coached his friends perfectly. "Stay bunched up!" he shouted. "Use the slipstream!"

Genji and Thea rode close behind Harrison as he sped ahead of the **Sharks** on the inside lane.

"Why are the **Sharks** in lane two?" Thea yelled to the others.

"Yikes—there's something on the track!" Harrison cried as he spotted some small stones. He veered away, warning his friends.

The girls followed close behind in the second lane, narrowly missing the stones, but they lost speed.

In the next second, two **Sharks** riders stormed in front. Harrison pedalled faster, narrowly ducking into the inside lane, again getting ahead of the **Sharks**. Thea and Genji followed. The **Sharks** edged closer behind Harrison.

Lap after lap they raced. Their wheels were blurred discs; their bodies hugging their steering wheels; their bikes jerking from side to side as the riders pumped their legs.

"Look out, Genji!" cried Thea behind her. Leo nearly clipped her back wheel.

Genji pedalled faster. Surprised, Leo lost his balance, and Genji and Thea soared into the inside lane ahead of him. The **Sharks** grunted, furious that they had handed over the inside lane.

Harrison and his team flashed past the winning flag, proudly waved by Carl's dad. The **Raiders** threw their hands into the air.

Harrison jumped off his bike. "We did it!" he panted, grinning from ear to ear. "We beat the **Sharks**!"

Genji, Thea and Harrison raced over to Carl and threw their arms around him. Carl's dad's voice boomed over the track. "Everyone, I present to you the winners!"

People cheered. Cameras flashed. Reporters rushed to interview the **Raiders**.

11 October

Ramsden Raiders Rule

In a nail-biting finish, the Ramsden Raiders, coached by Carl Hedron, rode to the finish line, just beating the Sharks led by Leo Humphries ...